Pudgy Possum and the Porcupine

Written and Illustrated by Kathy S. Elasky

ISBN 978-0-578-66413-2

Monday Creek Publishing LLC
mondaycreekpublishing.com

For Aryah and Bill. Thanks for your help and support.

Pudgy Possum loved pears. One evening, at the pear tree, he met someone new. A strange creature waddled up to him. It looked like a possum with sticks on its back.

"Hi, I'm Pudgy. I've never seen you before," said the possum.

"My name is Peter," the stranger replied. "Is this your tree?"

"No, just my favorite place to eat unless Felix Fox is around," Pudgy stated.

"I haven't seen Felix. I think we're safe and there are plenty of pears."

"Thank you," said Peter. "I'm not afraid of a fox." He started munching on a pear.

"Why not?" Pudgy asked.

"It's these quills. I'm a porcupine," Peter answered. "If a fox gets quills in his nose he'll be in pain for days. He leaves me alone."

"*Wow!*" Pudgy exclaimed. "I wish I had quills."

"I have to keep turning around so my quills are pointed at the fox though," responded Peter. "Anyway, thanks for sharing the pears."

Peter waddled off.

Oh, how Pudgy wished he had quills!

Pudgy suddenly had an idea and ran to the creek.

Once there, Pudgy gathered some small sticks. He dipped a stick into the mud. Next, he twisted the stick into his fur. It worked! The stick looked like Peter's quills.

Pudgy fixed sticks all over his back. He looked at his reflection in the water. He saw a porcupine! "Now I can go to the pear tree and not worry about the fox," Pudgy declared. Pudgy waddled off, just as he had seen Peter waddle.

Later, while munching on pears, Pudgy heard Felix Fox sneaking through the tall grass. Pudgy hoped the sticks would make Felix think he was a porcupine.

Felix came out of the grass. He sniffed at Pudgy.

"This smells like a possum but it looks sort of like a porcupine."

As Felix walked around him, Pudgy turned and kept his quills toward the fox. "I'm not sure about this," said Felix. "But, I'm so hungry I'll try a little nibble." Felix's mouth snapped shut! Pudgy felt some fur being pulled from his skin!

"*Ow*!" Felix cried. A fake quill was stuck between his teeth. "I'll need help to pull this out. I'll be back to eat whatever this is." Off he trotted.

Pudgy didn't want to be a fox dinner so he ran for his life, straight to the creek. He washed all the mud and sticks out of his fur. The sticks had saved his life, but Pudgy didn't like being tasted by Felix.

Next, Pudgy ran for home. He was too scared to come outside for days. Eventually, Pudgy got very hungry so he went back to the pear tree.

While he was eating pears, a noise scared Pudgy.

Whew, it was only Peter Porcupine not Felix Fox!

"I'm glad to see you again," Peter told Pudgy.

"I have an idea for how you could get some qui...."

"No thanks," Pudgy interrupted. "I'm better off just being me!

Fun fact: The opossum, commonly called possum, is North America's only marsupial. A marsupial is an animal with a pouch. For more information about opossums, go to opossumsocietyus.org.

About the Author

Kathy S. Elasky is a retired teacher/counselor from Southeast Ohio. She lives on a small farm with her husband, three dogs, one cat, several squirrels and the occasional raccoon or possum. She loves her family, church activities, nature, reading, crafting of all sorts and, of course, writing.